One of the frogs was holding a stick.
"What's that for?" asked the other frog.

"For protection," said the frog with the stick.

TWO FROGS

Chris Wormell

Red Fox

ONCE THERE WERE TWO FROGS sitting on a lily pad
in the middle of a large pond.

"This stick is to beat off the dog."

"What dog?" said the other frog, quickly looking over his shoulder. "I can't see a dog. There is no dog!"

"Not now there isn't, not at this moment," replied the frog with the stick. "But what if a dog should come swimming across the pond and try to eat us up? Better safe than sorry."

The other frog was puzzled. "But no dogs ever come swimming in this pond," he protested. "At least I've never seen one. In fact I can't even remember seeing one on the

edge of the pond. And why would a dog want to come swimming in the pond anyway? They're not so fond of swimming as us frogs, you know."

"Perhaps the dog's master might throw a ball out into the pond for him to fetch," suggested the frog with the stick.

"But this is such a large pond it would have to be a mighty throw to reach us out here," declared the other frog.

"And the dog would have to be a very good swimmer!"

"But suppose the dog's master was a champion javelin thrower?" suggested the frog with the stick. "Suppose a champion javelin thrower came to this pond with his dog (who was an excellent swimmer) and

threw the ball right out here to the middle for his dog to fetch. And what if the dog, while fetching the ball, came upon us frogs and tried to eat us up? Well, I have a stick to beat off the dog!"

The other frog burst out laughing. "Foolish frog!" he cried. "You're much more likely to be eaten by a pike or a heron than by a dog. Why worry about dogs? It's ridiculous!"

He laughed so much he fell into the pond.

Just at that moment, a large pike was swimming by
beneath the lily pads.

It heard the plop of the frog falling in...

It opened its enormous toothy jaws and was just

about to gobble up the two frogs...

when a heron snapped them up in its beak.

It flew off, leaving the large pike chewing on a lily pad.

But...

the stick jammed in the heron's beak as it tried to swallow the two frogs.

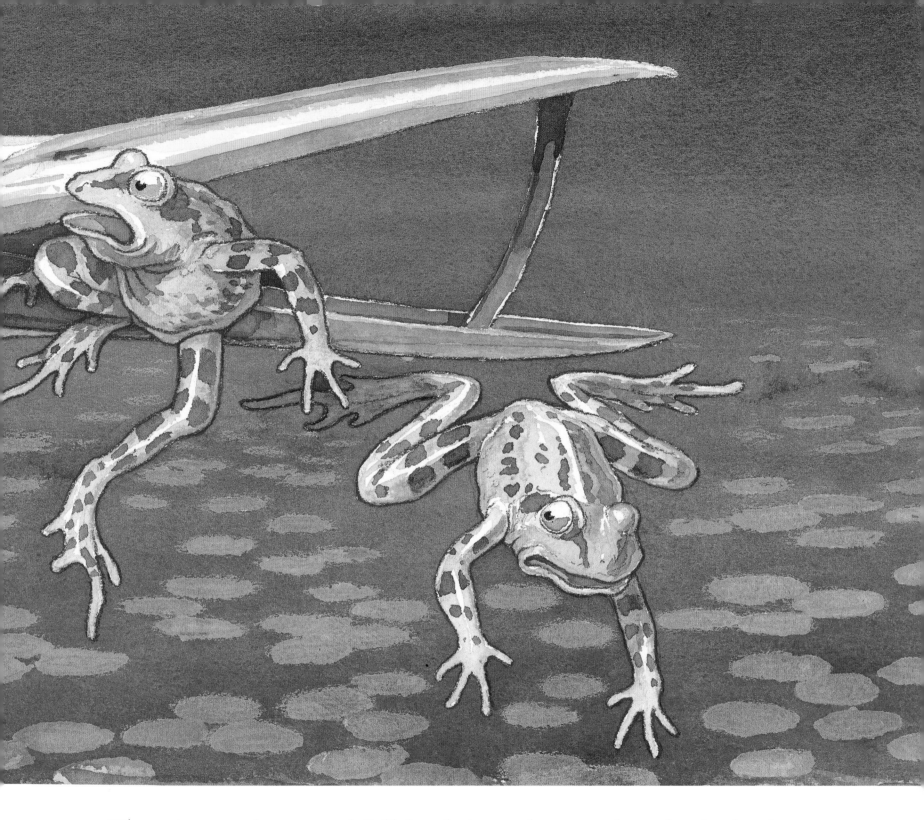

They jumped out and fell back into the pond – plop! plop!

As soon as they hit the water the two frogs swam as fast as they could

to the shore and hopped off into the woods looking for sticks.

So they missed the champion javelin thrower who came

to the pond that morning with his dog...

For Jack and Mary

TWO FROGS
A RED FOX BOOK 0 09 9438623

First published in Great Britain by Jonathan Cape,
an imprint of Random House Children's Books

Jonathan Cape edition published 2003
Red Fox edition published 2003

3 5 7 9 10 8 6 4 2

Red Fox Books are published by Random House Children's Books,
61—63 Uxbridge Road, London W5 5SA,
a division of The Random House Group Ltd,
in Australia by Random House Australia (Pty) Ltd,
20 Alfred Street, Milsons Point, Sydney, NSW 2061, Australia,
in New Zealand by Random House New Zealand Ltd,
18 Poland Road, Glenfield, Auckland 10, New Zealand,
and in South Africa by Random House (Pty) Ltd,
Endulini, 5A Jubilee Road, Parktown 2193, South Africa

THE RANDOM HOUSE GROUP Limited Reg. No. 954009
www.kidsatrandomhouse.co.uk

A CIP catalogue record for this book is available from the British Library.

Printed in Hong Kong